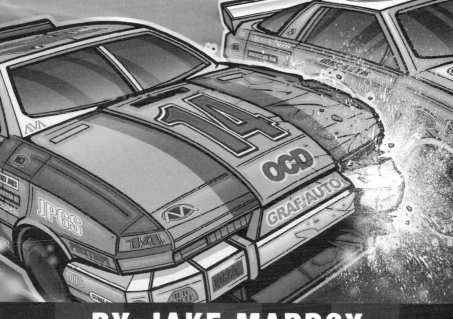

STOCK CAR SABOTAGE

BY JAKE MADDOX

illustrated by Sean Tiffany

text by Eric Stevens

STONE ARCH BOOKS
www.stonearchbooks.com

Impact Books are published by Stone Arch Books
151 Good Counsel Drive, P.O. Box 669
Mankato, Minnesota 56002
www.stonearchbooks.com

Library of Congress Cataloging-in-Publication Data
Maddox, Jake.
    Stock car sabotage / by Jake Maddox; text by Eric Stevens;
    illustrated by Sean Tiffany.
    p. cm. — (Impact books. A Jake Maddox sports story
    (on the speedway))
    ISBN 978-1-4342-1603-8 (library binding)
    [1. Stock car racing—Fiction. 2. Automobile racing—Fiction.]
I. Stevens, Eric, 1974– II. Tiffany, Sean, ill. III. Title.
PZ7.M25643Stj 2010
[Fic]—dc22   2009004291

Creative Director: Heather Kindseth
Graphic Designer: Hilary Wacholz

TABLE OF CONTENTS

CHAPTER 1

"CLEAN" COLE MASON

In garage 9 at the River City Raceway, Danny Mason pushed a broom across the floor. He wasn't doing much good sweeping though. His attention was on the TV monitors that lined the walls. "Come on, Cole!" he shouted at the TVs.

Danny's older brother, "Clean" Cole Mason, was driving car 9. Today's race was the River City classic. Cole had to do well if he hoped to win the series of races.

Now he was in third place. It was good enough to stay high in overall league standings. But Danny still hoped his brother would come in first.

Before long, the checkered flag was waving as Harvey Nickel in car 14 drove across the finish line. Close behind him was Scott Stanley in car 11.

Clean Cole Mason came in third.

"Darn!" Danny said to himself. Still, Cole had done well. He was one of the best racers on the regional circuit. If he kept racing the way he had for the last few months, he'd make it to NASCAR for sure.

Danny dropped the broom. He jogged out of the garage to wave at his brother as car 9 pulled in.

The car came to a stop in the garage.

Some of the pit crew helped Cole climb out. "Great race, Cole!" Danny called out. He gave his brother a high five.

"Thanks, bro," Cole said. He pulled off his helmet. He was smiling, but Danny could tell his brother wasn't feeling very happy.

"Are you disappointed about coming in third?" Danny asked.

Cole shook his head slowly. "Harvey Nickel," he said. "He's just too good."

"You haven't been able to beat him this series, have you?" Danny asked.

"No," Cole answered. "I mean, Scott Stanley is no big deal. I think we're well matched. I outrace him sometimes, and he outraces me sometimes. But Harvey . . . I just can't seem to pass him."

"Do you think he has a better machine?" Danny asked.

He had noticed that a lot of the guys in the pit crews said "machine" when they talked about cars. Danny wanted to sound like all of the other guys.

"I think our machines are about even," Cole replied.

"Maybe you should let me on the pit crew!" Danny said. "I'll cut your pit time in half."

Cole laughed. "You know you're too young to be in the pit crew, Danny," he said. "You're only fourteen. Wait a couple of years."

Danny shrugged. "It was worth a shot," he said. "So why does Harvey keep winning?"

Cole put a gloved hand on his little brother's shoulder. "Some drivers," he said, "are just better than others. But, boy, I'd do just about anything to beat him once."

CHAPTER 2

THE EIGHTH MAN

The following weekend, race time came around again. This time, the Mason boys were at the Lakeville Speedway.

"You ready to race, Cole?" Danny asked.

Cole pulled on his helmet as the pit crew pushed car 9 out of the garage.

"Sure am, Danny," Cole replied. "I have a really good feeling about the race today. I just know I'm going to beat Harvey Nickel this time."

Danny patted his brother on the back and headed into the garage to watch the race on the TV monitors.

About halfway through the race, Danny stood in the garage. He was leaning on his push broom, staring at the monitors.

He watched car 9, Clean Cole's car. Cole was driving hard, but just like last week, he couldn't pass Harvey Nickel.

Suddenly, Danny felt a hand on his shoulder. He turned.

It was Jim Yolk, one of the new guys on Cole's pit crew. Danny knew that Jim was the eighth man on the crew.

Normally, only seven men were allowed over the wall and onto the track during a pit stop. Sometimes, though, an eighth man could go over.

The eighth man wasn't allowed to do everything. He could only do things like bring water for the driver or clean the windshield.

Most of the time, though, Jim didn't have anything to do during a pit stop.

Jim was a tall, broad man, and he smiled all the time. It wasn't a nice smile, though. It was creepy. Danny thought there was something weird about him.

"Hi, Danny," Jim said.

"Hi," Danny replied.

"Your brother is really giving his all out there today," Jim went on, glancing at the TV monitors.

"I guess so," Danny said. "He already has Scott Stanley beat. I know he wants to beat Harvey Nickel, too."

Jim winked. "He sure does," he said. "I'd say he'd do just about anything to beat Harvey Nickel, wouldn't you?"

Danny shrugged. "I don't know," he said. He thought about it for a moment. "Well, I don't think he'd do *anything*."

Jim patted Danny's shoulder and turned to leave. "Well, don't worry too much," Jim said. "I have a feeling he's going to win this race."

With that, Jim Yolk headed back to his place with the pit crew.

Danny watched the rest of the race closely. With three laps to go, Harvey was still in first place, and Cole was still in second. They led the pack by a long way, but Cole was no closer to getting around Harvey.

"I guess Jim was wrong," Danny mumbled to himself.

But suddenly, as Harvey came around a curve, his engine cut out completely. Car 14 just rolled to a stop!

Danny gasped as Cole sped toward the stopped car. His brother was a great driver. He was able to steer around the stopped car and take the lead.

But the third-place driver, Lou Dyver in car 5, couldn't swerve in time. He rear-ended Harvey's car, sending both cars into the wall!

CHAPTER 3

AN ACCIDENT?

After the crash, the warning flag came down right away, and the other drivers slowed to a stop. Moments later, Harvey and Lou climbed out of their cars and waved to the crowd. They were both okay, but out of the race.

Danny sighed with relief. "At least no one was hurt," he said to himself.

Soon the race started again, with only two laps to go. Cole won easily.

Car 9 pulled into the garage. Danny watched as the crowd went crazy.

"How about that, Danny?" Cole said after he climbed out of the car. "Lucky break, huh?"

Danny scratched his chin. "For you, sure," he said. "Not so lucky for Harvey, though."

Cole laughed. "That's true," he said. "He's not hurt, though, so it's okay." Cole mussed Danny's hair and walked off to change.

Danny frowned. He wasn't so sure it was okay.

He strolled down the infield until he saw Eddie Paulsen. Eddie worked on Lou Dyver's pit crew. He was the Dyver crew's jack man, the toughest job on the crew.

It was Eddie's job to get the car up off the ground quickly during a pit stop so the tire changers could do their work. It wasn't an easy job.

The scariest part was when the car pulled in. The jack man had to run to the side of the car as the driver pulled in — heading right at him!

Danny didn't think he would ever have the nerve to run across the path of a speeding car. He would be too nervous that the driver wouldn't stop in time and he would be run over.

"Hi, Eddie," Danny said. "Some race!"

"Some ending, you mean!" Eddie replied. "Lou hasn't been in the top three in about ten races. He's angry he lost his third-place finish at the last second."

"I don't blame him," Danny replied. "I'd be angry too."

Danny glanced around to make sure no one else was listening. Then he leaned closer to Eddie. "Did the accident seem sort of weird to you?" Danny asked.

"What do you mean?" Eddie asked.

"Well, I was talking to Jim Yolk during the race," Danny explained. "You know Jim. The new guy on my brother's pit crew."

Eddie nodded. "Sure," he said. "I've known Jim Yolk for years. Not very well, though."

"Anyway, Jim said he was sure Cole would beat Harvey in the race," Danny went on. "Even though Cole had been behind the whole race. Plus, he's never beaten Harvey. Ever!"

"Well, he is on Cole's pit crew," Eddie said with a shrug. "Of course he wants your brother to win."

"But he was so sure Cole would win," Danny said. "It was like he knew he would win somehow. Like he knew the accident would happen."

Eddie leaned back and waved his arms. "Whoa, whoa," he said. "Are you saying Jim Yolk had something to do with Harvey's machine stalling?"

Danny scratched his chin. "Don't you think it's possible?" he asked.

Eddie smiled. "I guess it might be possible," he said. "But sometimes machines have problems. You can't just start pointing fingers."

"I guess you're right," Danny said.

"Besides," Eddie added quickly, "your brother didn't earn the nickname 'Clean' Cole by hiring shady guys to work in his pit crew. If Cole likes Jim Yolk, he must be a good guy."

Danny had to agree with that. His brother was the nicest, fairest guy on the circuit. There was no way he'd hire anyone who would make an opponent crash. Was there?

CHAPTER 4

LUCKY BREAK?

The next afternoon, Cole and Danny were hanging out in their garage at home. Cole tinkered with an old sports car he had been restoring, while Danny helped as much as he could.

"I can't wait to get this machine running," Cole said, looking under the hood of the car.

The car had been built in the 1960s. It was small and sleek and silver.

Cole had gotten it for a steal when he was only sixteen. But he'd been working on it for three years, and the motor still didn't turn over.

"It's going to be awesome," Danny agreed. He couldn't wait to get his own driver's license.

"So, Cole," Danny said. Cole continued to work under the hood of his car. "That was some lucky break you got yesterday, huh?"

"Huh?" Cole said. "Lucky break? What do you mean?"

"In the race," Danny added. "When Harvey stalled and then Lou Dyver hit him."

Cole chuckled. "Oh, that," he said. "Yeah, I guess it was lucky."

"Does Harvey's crew know what happened?" Danny said. "Or do the race officials know what caused the stall?"

Cole shrugged and walked over to his tool box. "Who knows?" he said. "Listen, Danny. In this game, sometimes things go wrong. People crash. Machines stall."

Cole picked up a rag and wiped some grease from his hands.

"I guess so," Danny agreed.

"Besides," Cole went on, "I was going to pass Harvey, stall or not. I knew I was going to win that race."

"You did?" Danny asked. "How did you know?"

"I could just feel it, that's all," Cole replied. "Now let's get some lunch, okay?"

Danny followed his brother to the house. "Sure, Cole," he said. But as he walked into the house, he thought, *How did Cole know he would win? He hasn't beaten Harvey all year.*

CHAPTER 5

CRYING JIM YOLK

The next race was held at Willow Junction Speedway. As the teams and drivers were getting ready, Jim walked over to Danny.

"Told you Cole would win last week, didn't I?" Jim asked Danny.

Danny looked Jim right in the eyes. "Yes, you did," he replied. "You were very certain."

Jim laughed. "I sure was," he said. "You might say I knew that Harvey wouldn't be able to finish."

"Did you know Harvey Nickel was going to stall and get into a crash?" Danny asked.

Jim smirked. "Now, how would I have known something like that?" he asked. "I mean, I can't predict the future or something, can I?"

Danny was about to agree. But then Jim winked.

Then, with another sly smile, Jim turned and walked away.

* * *

"Eddie!" Danny cried out. He ran through the infield toward Lou Dyver's garage. "Eddie, where are you?"

"Whoa, there, Danny," Eddie said as he stepped out of the Dyver garage. "What's all the hollering about?"

"Eddie," Danny said as he caught his breath. "It's Jim Yolk."

Eddie rolled his eyes. "Danny, have you ever heard of the boy who cried wolf?" he asked.

"I'm not crying wolf," Danny replied. "I'm crying Jim Yolk."

"Okay, so what happened now?" Eddie asked. He crossed his arms.

"Jim just strolled right up to me and admitted he knew for sure that Cole would win last week," Danny explained.

"Didn't we go over this last weekend?" Eddie said.

"There's more," Danny said. "When I asked if Jim knew that Harvey would stall, Jim said, 'How would I have known that?' Then he winked!"

Eddie burst out laughing. "Winked?" he said through his laughter. "That's your big evidence? A wink?"

"Don't you see?" Danny protested. "The wink meant he did know, but it's a secret."

Eddie glanced at his watch. "Look, Danny," he said. "The race is going to start soon. You better get back to your brother's garage."

"You don't believe me," Danny said.

Eddie patted Danny's shoulder. "You shouldn't watch those detective shows on TV," he said. "They're messing with your mind." Then he turned and walked off.

Danny was disappointed. He was certain Jim had something to do with the crash, but even Eddie didn't believe him. Feeling low, Danny headed back toward the Mason garage.

As he was leaving, he heard Lou Dyver talking to Harvey Nickel. Harvey wasn't in his racing gear.

"So you're not racing today, Harv?" Lou asked.

Harvey shook his head. "Nope," he replied. "The team doctor wants me to sit this week out because of the accident. It's nothing serious, but he says I should take a week off."

"That's too bad," Lou said. "Any word on what caused that stall? Really left us both in the dust, huh?"

"Sure did," Harvey replied. "It looks like there was some water in the fuel line."

"That'll do it," Lou said. "How'd you get water in your fuel?"

Harvey shrugged. "You got me," he said. "But for that amount of water to get into my fuel, something funny must have gone on."

Danny had heard enough. Now he was certain someone had messed with Harvey's car to make it stall.

And I bet a million dollars it was Jim Yolk, he thought.

CHAPTER 6

IN THE BAG

When Danny got back to the Mason garage, Cole was just putting his helmet on.

"Do you think you have a good shot at winning this race, Cole?" Danny asked.

"I sure do," Cole replied. Together, the brothers walked over to car 9 so Cole could climb in. "With Harvey taking the week off," Cole went on, "I'm feeling pretty certain I'll win this race."

"What about Scott Stanley?" Danny asked.

"I've beaten him lots of times," Cole replied. "I'm feeling good."

"And what about Lou Dyver?" Danny added.

"Lou Dyver?" Cole said back. "He's never even come in the top three. He's no threat."

"Last week he was in the top three," Danny pointed out, "until the crash."

"I guess that's how it goes," Cole said. "I'll tell you what. I'll watch out for Lou, if you stop worrying about everything. I've got this race in the bag."

Cole climbed into the car, and his crew rolled it out of the garage. The race was about to start.

Danny watched the cars line up for the start of the race. The engines revved and the crowd went wild.

Jim Yolk brushed past Danny on his way to the pit.

"Hey, Jim," Danny said. He grabbed the man by the arm.

"Oh, hi, Danny," Jim replied with a smile. It gave Danny the chills. "What's up?"

"So do you think Cole will win the race today?" Danny asked.

Jim's smile got even bigger. "Let's just say I have a very, very good feeling about it," he said.

Then he reached into the pocket of his jumpsuit and pulled something out.

He held it in front of Danny for a moment, then tossed it into the air and caught it. It was a shiny metal thing, with three holes. Danny stared at the object for a moment. It looked like a short, two-headed pipe.

"Well, I better get to the pit," Jim said. He shoved the object back into his pocket. Then, with a wink at Danny, he turned and walked off.

CHAPTER 7

NOT SO CLEAN?

Scott Stanley and Cole drove hard the whole race. Stanley really wanted to win, but so did Cole.

Danny watched the monitors the whole race. With only a few laps to go, Cole and Stanley both went into the pits.

The Cole Mason pit crew leaped into action. They gave car 9 more fuel and four new tires. Danny watched closely. He didn't see Jim Yolk go near the car at all.

In about fifteen seconds, car 9 was already finished in the pit. The seven crewmen pushed the car out as far as they were allowed.

Cole's car and Scott Stanley's car were neck and neck as they rejoined the main track.

Suddenly, though, in the last lap, Scott Stanley's engine cut off. Stanley was able to ease his car into the infield. Meanwhile, Cole sped on to the finish line and the checkered flag.

Back in the garage, Danny watched the monitors. He could hardly believe his eyes! Another car had stalled, and once again, it had given his brother first place.

Something weird was definitely going on. Someone had to believe him now.

Danny decided to find Eddie. He hadn't believed Danny before, but now he would.

As Danny ran out of the garage, car 9 pulled in. His brother Cole was at the wheel, cheering.

"Another win," Danny said, but he wasn't smiling.

"Darn right," Cole replied. He climbed out of the car. "I have a shot at winning this series now, you know that?"

"Why did Stanley's car stall?" Danny asked.

"Who knows?" Cole replied. "This was a big race. His crew probably choked."

"Maybe," Danny said.

"All I know is I'm having a great run of luck," Cole added.

Someone called to Cole. He patted his brother on the back and strode off.

"Yeah, luck," Danny mumbled to himself. "If you can call it that."

* * *

"Eddie!" Danny said as he jogged up to the Dyver garage.

"I had a feeling I'd see you pretty soon," Eddie said quietly. "I think I'm ready to listen to you now."

"Good," Danny said.

Then he told Eddie about his meeting with Jim before the race. He described the funny metal thing Jim had put in his pocket.

Eddie nodded slowly. "Sounds like a hose splitter," he said. "That makes sense."

"Should we tell an official?" Danny asked. "Or call the police? Or something?"

"Slow down," Eddie said. "There's a right way and a wrong way to deal with this."

Eddie sat down on the metal bench in his team's garage. "I just can't believe your brother would let this happen," he said with a sigh. "I mean, he's Clean Cole Mason. He's the most honest guy in the league."

Danny scratched his chin. "Well," he said, "maybe he didn't let it happen. Jim's the newest guy on the crew. No one knows him that well."

"You think maybe he did this without your brother knowing?" Eddie asked.

Danny stared at his brother's garage. "I sure hope so," he said.

CHAPTER 8

CHEATING FOR SURE

Back at the Mason garage, Danny found Cole changing out of his racing jumpsuit.

"Hey, Danny," Cole said. "Where have you been?"

"I was just talking to Eddie, over at Lou Dyver's garage," Danny replied. He sat down on the bench along the wall.

"I always liked Eddie Paulsen," Cole said. "One of the best jack men in the sport. Nice guy, too."

"He called you the most honest guy in the league," Danny said.

"Did he?" Cole said. He turned to his little brother and looked him square in the eye. "That's nice. What were you two talking about, anyway?"

Danny took a deep breath. Was he really about to ask his brother if he was a cheater?

"I don't know how to say this," Danny said. "We think Jim sabotaged Scott's car today and Harvey's car last week."

Cole was stunned. "You think Jim is cheating?" he asked. "I can't believe one of my crewmen would ever do anything like that."

"That's what I thought, and Eddie too," Danny replied. "But now I'm sure of it."

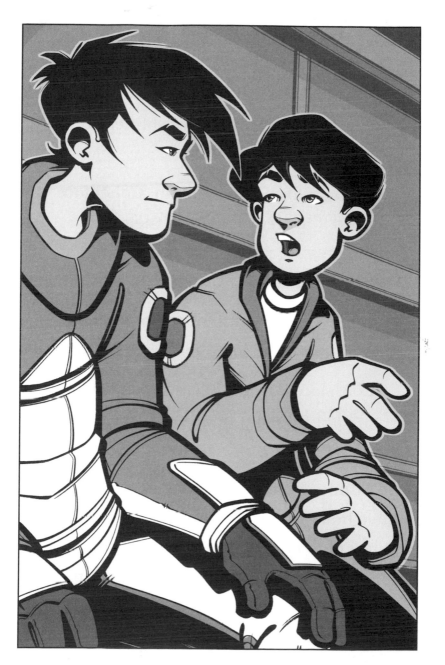

"How can you be so sure?" Cole asked.

"Jim pretty much told me," Danny said. "He even showed me a hose splitter he keeps in his pocket."

As the information sank in, Cole's face dropped. "To feed water into their fuel lines," he said quietly. "Of course. That's what happened."

"Then . . . ," Danny stammered, "you didn't know anything about this, did you?"

Cole stared at his little brother. "Danny, you didn't think I'd put Jim up to this, did you?" he asked.

Danny shrugged. "I knew you couldn't have had anything to do with it," he said. "I just didn't know how a shady guy like Jim could have been added to the team without you knowing it."

Cole sighed. Then he looked at his brother. "We have to catch Jim in the act," Cole said. "We need proof."

"If you don't mind waiting until next week's race," Danny said, "I think I have a plan."

CHAPTER 9

THE PLAN

The next weekend, all the teams were at the South Downs Super Speedway. This race was one of the longest of the series. Most drivers thought it was the most important race of the year.

"Harvey's back on the track today," Cole said. He and Danny were hanging out in the Mason garage before the race. "He and Scott Stanley are the big competition today."

"And Lou Dyver," Danny put in.

Cole laughed. "And Lou Dyver," he agreed.

"I wonder who Jim Yolk will hit this week, then," Danny said. "Harvey Nickel, probably."

Cole shook his head and stood up. "Hopefully no one, if your plan works, right?"

Danny smiled. "Right," he said. "Now you better get ready and get going. Jim might show up any time."

"I hope this works, Danny," Cole said. "When Jim gets caught, I want Team Mason to be the ones to catch him."

Cole pulled on his helmet. The pit crew — except for Jim — came in and pushed car 9 out of the garage. Cole followed.

Danny was alone in the garage, with the monitors, tools, and benches. And a new closed-circuit TV camera.

He was nervous. He knew Cole was really counting on him. The whole team was counting on him. In some ways, even the whole league was counting on him. If Jim's cheating wasn't stopped soon, the whole sport could be tainted.

Danny watched the TV monitors lining the garage walls. He saw Harvey Nickel's car pull up to the start line. Lou Dyver and Scott Stanley were close behind, along with his brother's car.

There was still no sign of Jim Yolk when the race started.

Right away, Harvey Nickel sped off into the lead. Cole stayed right on him.

During the next fifty laps, the two excellent drivers swapped first and second place over and over.

Lou Dyver and Scott Stanley fought it out for third place. Both drivers struggled to stay in the top three, but the leaders were well ahead.

"I guess Harvey is the man to beat today," a voice suddenly said.

Danny spun around. It was Jim Yolk.

"Oh, hi, Jim," Danny said with a little stutter. "I didn't hear you come in."

Jim stood next to Danny and looked at the monitors. "Some race, huh?" Jim said. "A real close one. The top four drivers are really giving it their all."

"Who do you think will come out on top?" Danny asked.

Jim chuckled. "It's not who I think will win that matters," he said. "It's who I know will win. Know what I mean?"

Danny scratched his chin. "No," he said. "What do you mean?"

Jim smiled slyly. "Oh, come on, Danny boy," he said. "You know what I mean."

Jim reached into his pocket and pulled out the hose splitter. He held it up for Danny to get a good look at.

"You know what this is?" Jim asked.

Danny shrugged. "A hose splitter, isn't it?" he asked.

Jim nodded. "That's right," he said. "This is what's going to make sure your older brother and Team Mason are number one this year."

Danny glanced at the camera mounted in the corner. He hoped Jim wouldn't notice it, not until he confessed completely.

"That little thing?" Danny said. "I must be stupid or something, then. Because I'm watching the race and Harvey Nickel is still in first."

Jim glanced at the monitor. "He is now," he said. "But in a few more laps he'll enter pit lane. And when he does, I'll do my stuff."

That's not enough proof, Danny thought. Jim had said a lot already, but Danny wanted more on camera to be certain.

"What stuff do you mean?" Danny asked. He tried to sound calm and relaxed. He kept his eyes on the race, like he wasn't even interested in what Jim was saying.

"Can you keep a secret?" Jim asked with a grin. "This hose splitter lets me add a little something to any fuel line in the infield."

Danny finally looked away from the TVs and right at Jim Yolk. "What would you add?" he asked.

"Just a little water," Jim said. He was practically whispering. Danny wasn't sure the camera's small microphone would be able to pick up Jim's voice.

"To stall the engine," Danny finished. "Right? That's what would happen?"

Jim leaned back and grinned. Then he nodded. "Now you got it," he said. "Why, if it wasn't for me and my hose splitter, your brother might not even be in the top three right now."

Danny and Jim turned back to the monitors. Harvey Nickel was about to pull into the pit lane.

"Whoops, that's my cue," Jim said. He slipped the hose splitter back into his pocket. "I better get over to Nickel's fuel line and cinch this race for Clean Cole Mason."

Jim laughed as he turned to leave the garage. But he stopped laughing pretty quickly. Standing in the doorway of the garage were two security guards and a race official.

"Not so fast, Yolk," the official said. "You're busted."

CHAPTER 10

BUSTED

"We've been watching this whole conversation on video," the race official said. "Cole Mason himself tipped us off to your cheating, so we know you worked alone."

"Cole told you what I was doing?" Jim asked, stunned. "How did he even know?"

"Danny here figured it out," the official replied. "And he just got you to confess on camera."

The official motioned toward the men at his side. "Get him out of here!" he ordered.

The two security guards moved forward and took Jim Yolk by the arms. They escorted him out of the garage.

"Good going, Danny," the official said. He patted Danny on the back. "Your brother will be proud of you. You've really saved the name of Clean Cole."

* * *

Clean Cole Mason did finish first in that race, but not because Harvey Nickel couldn't compete. Nickel, Lou Dyver, and Scott Stanley all drove well. But Cole beat them all.

After the race, Cole pulled car 9 into the Mason garage. Danny was waiting there, cheering.

"You're the one who deserves the cheers, kid," Cole said. He climbed out of the car. "If it wasn't for you, Team Mason could have been run out of the sport. And now I'm pretty sure I will make it to NASCAR soon."

"I'm just sorry I ever suspected that you were involved with Jim's dirty work," Danny said.

"Don't worry about it," Cole replied. He threw an arm around his little brother's shoulders and added, "I should have kept a better eye on my crew."

Danny pointed at the camera in the corner. "Between me and the eye in the sky there," he said with a laugh, "I'd say we've got it covered."

ABOUT THE AUTHOR

Eric Stevens lives in St. Paul, Minnesota. He is studying to become a middle-school English teacher. Some of his favorite things include pizza, playing video games, watching cooking shows on TV, riding his bike, and trying new restaurants. Some of his least favorite things include olives and shoveling snow.

ABOUT THE ILLUSTRATOR

When Sean Tiffany was growing up, he lived on a small island off the coast of Maine. Every day, from sixth grade until he graduated from high school, he had to take a boat to get to school. When Sean isn't working on his art, he works on a multimedia project called "OilCan Drive," which combines music and art. He has a pet cactus named Jim.

GLOSSARY

competition (kom-puh-TISH-uhn)—a person you are trying to beat

evidence (EV-uh-duns)—information and facts that help prove something

opponent (uh-POH-nuhnt)—someone you compete against

predict (pri-DIKT)—to say what will happen in the future

restoring (ri-STOR-ing)—fixing an item so it is back in its original condition

sabotaged (SAB-uh-tahzhed)—caused damage to something on purpose

suspected (suh-SPEKT-id)—thought that someone was guilty with little or no proof

NASCAR

On track straightaways, NASCAR drivers can drive 293 feet in just one second. The distance is almost equal to that of a football field.

It's hot behind the wheel! Temperatures often reach more than 100 degrees inside the car.

All that heat makes them sweat! In a typical race, drivers lose five to ten pounds.

Drivers need to replace the fluids they lose in sweat. If he or she loses more than three percent of body weight, the driver's focus and reflexes will suffer.

FUN FACTS

During turns, NASCAR drivers feel incredible force against their bodies. When measured, the amount of force is similar to the amount of force an astronaut feels during shuttle liftoff.

According to research, being fit helps drivers. Muscle mass helps drivers handle the forces and provides more protection in crashes.

Driving a race is like running a marathon. During a race, a NASCAR driver's heart rate is between 120 and 150 beats per minute for more than three hours. Serious marathon runners maintain the same heart rates for roughly the same amount of time.

DISCUSSION QUESTIONS

1. Why didn't Eddie Paulsen believe Danny at first?

2. Danny looked up to his brother Cole. How do you think he felt when he thought that Cole might be cheating?

3. Cole was excited about his run of wins. How do you think he felt when he realized Jim had been tampering with the competitors' cars?

WRITING PROMPTS

1. Have you ever been to a car race? Write about it. Describe the sights, sounds, and even the smells at the track.

2. Write a news article that reports the events of the book.

3. At the end of chapter six, Jim is on his way to the pit with his hose splitter. Write a scene that describes what he does next.